I0752949

CARNAL

Dale Lazarov & theAmir

CARNAL

Script and art direction by Dale Lazarov
Linework and colors by theAmir

StickyGraphicNovels.com

Printed and distributed by
ComicMix, LLC.,
304 Main Avenue, Suite #194,
Norwalk, CT 06851.
http://www.comicmix.com

Printed in USA.

Hardcover ISBN: 978-1-939888-53-2

HUNK TANK

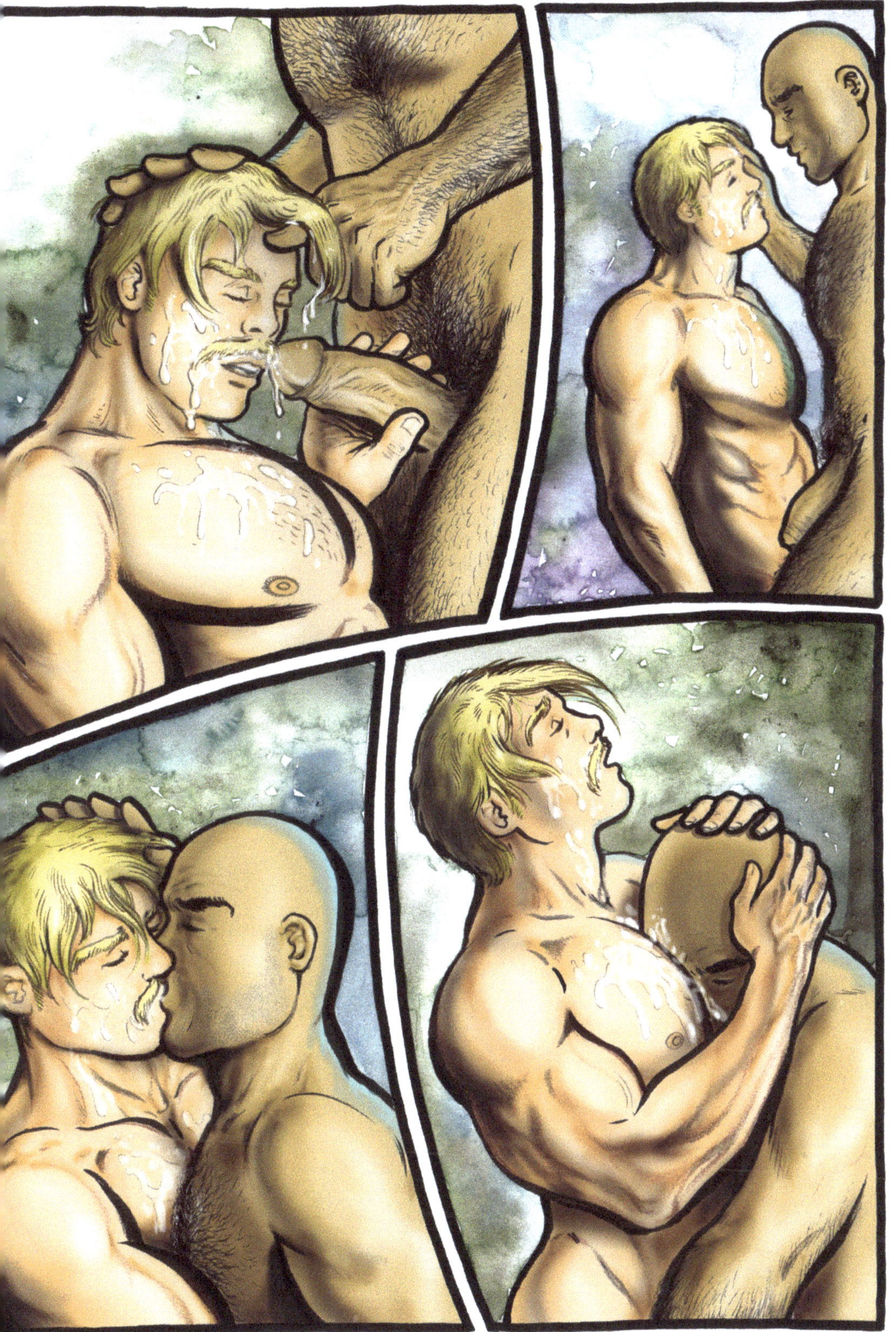

THE
AMIR

THE
AMIR

YOUR TURN

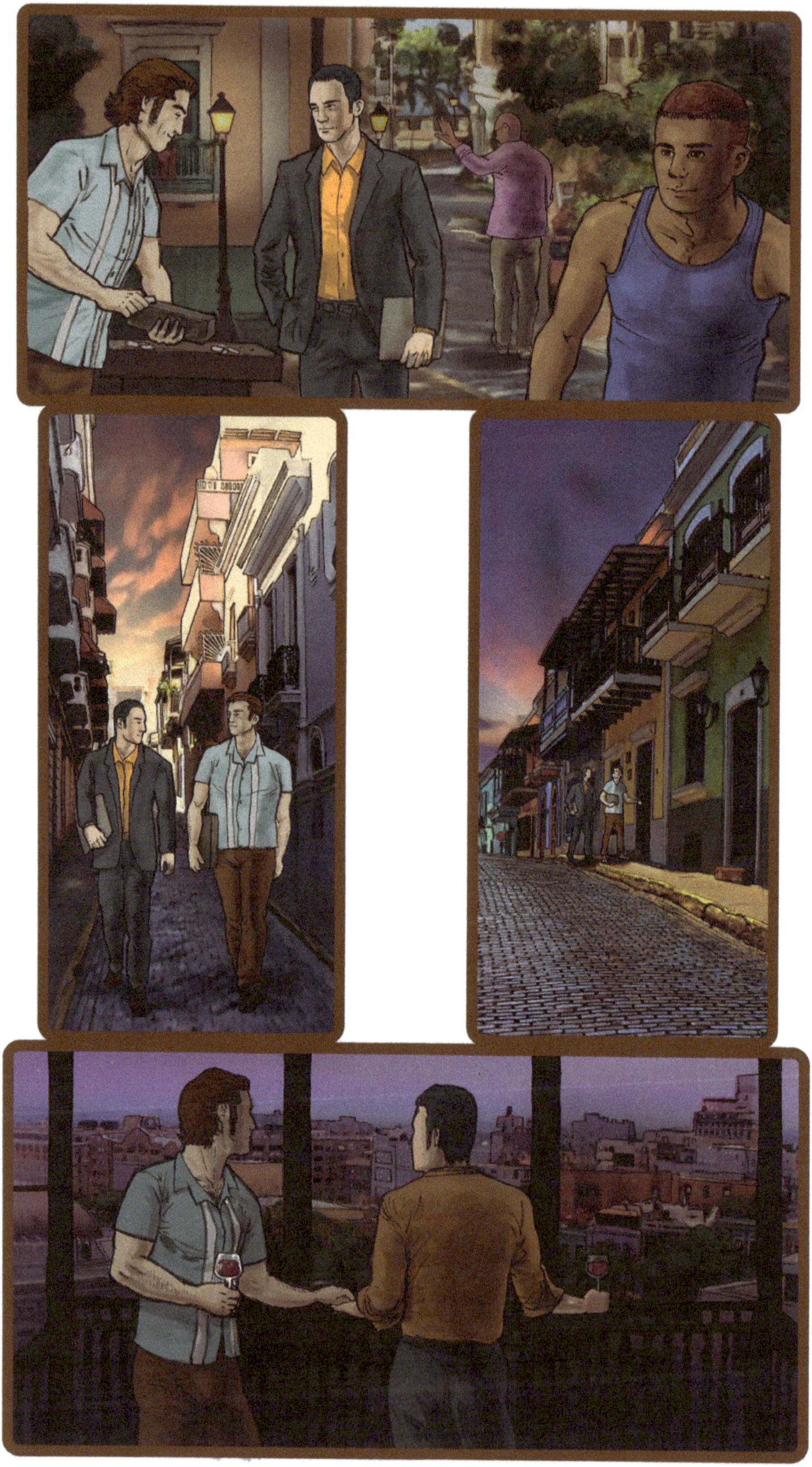

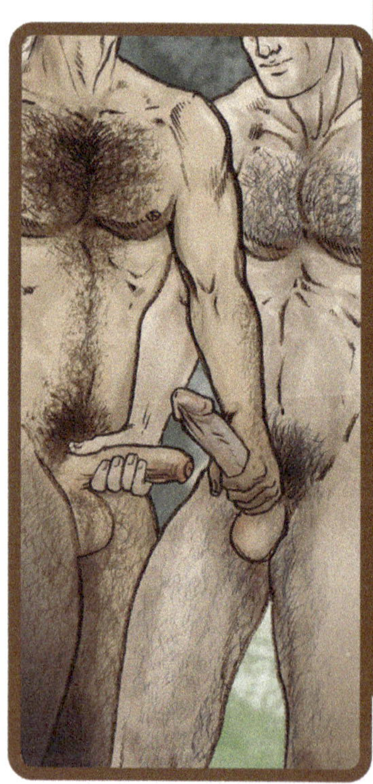

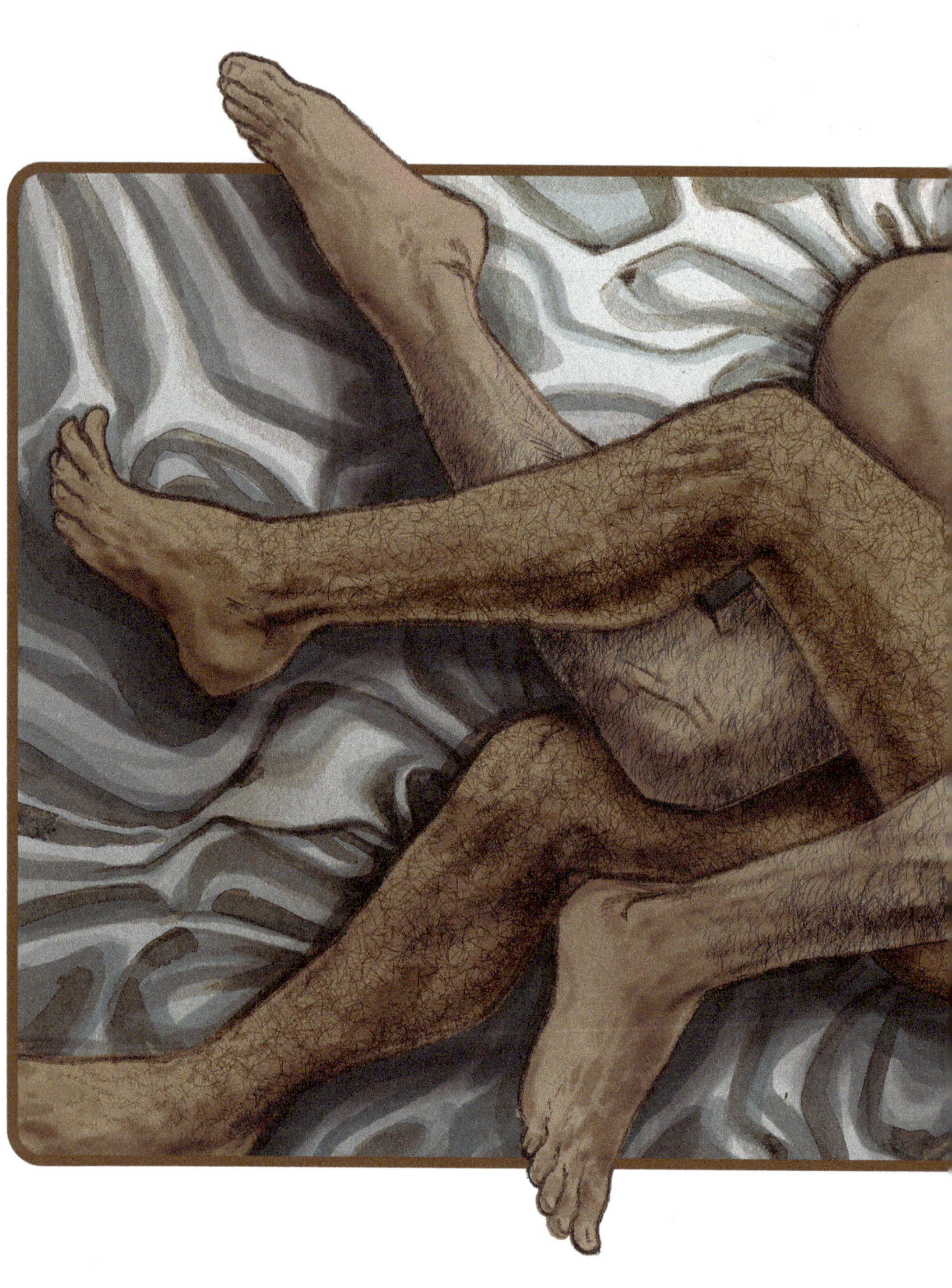

FIN

LAPTOP REPAI

THE AMIR
THE AMIR

THE AMIR

Saved Cam2Cam
Saved Cam2Cam

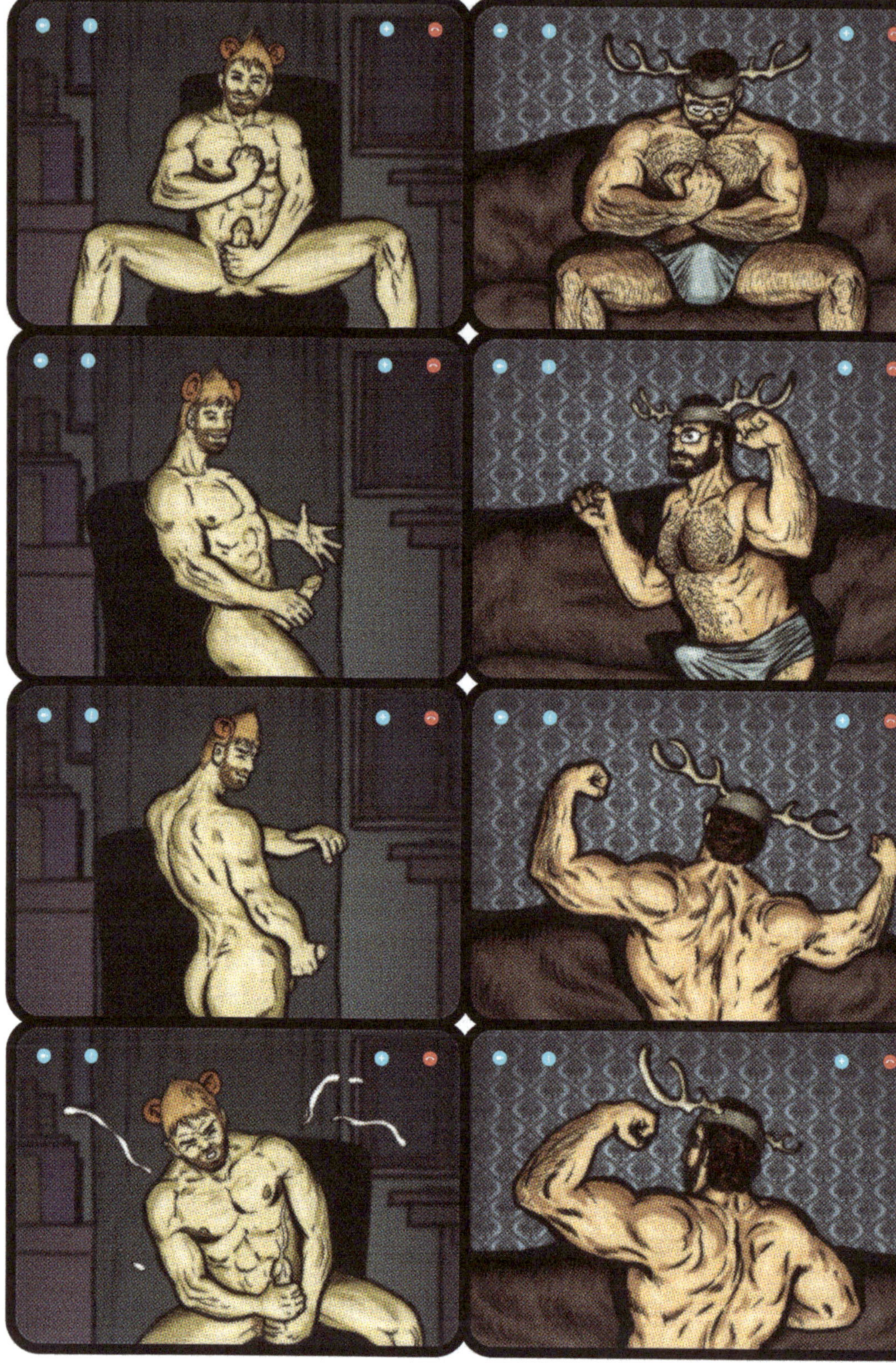

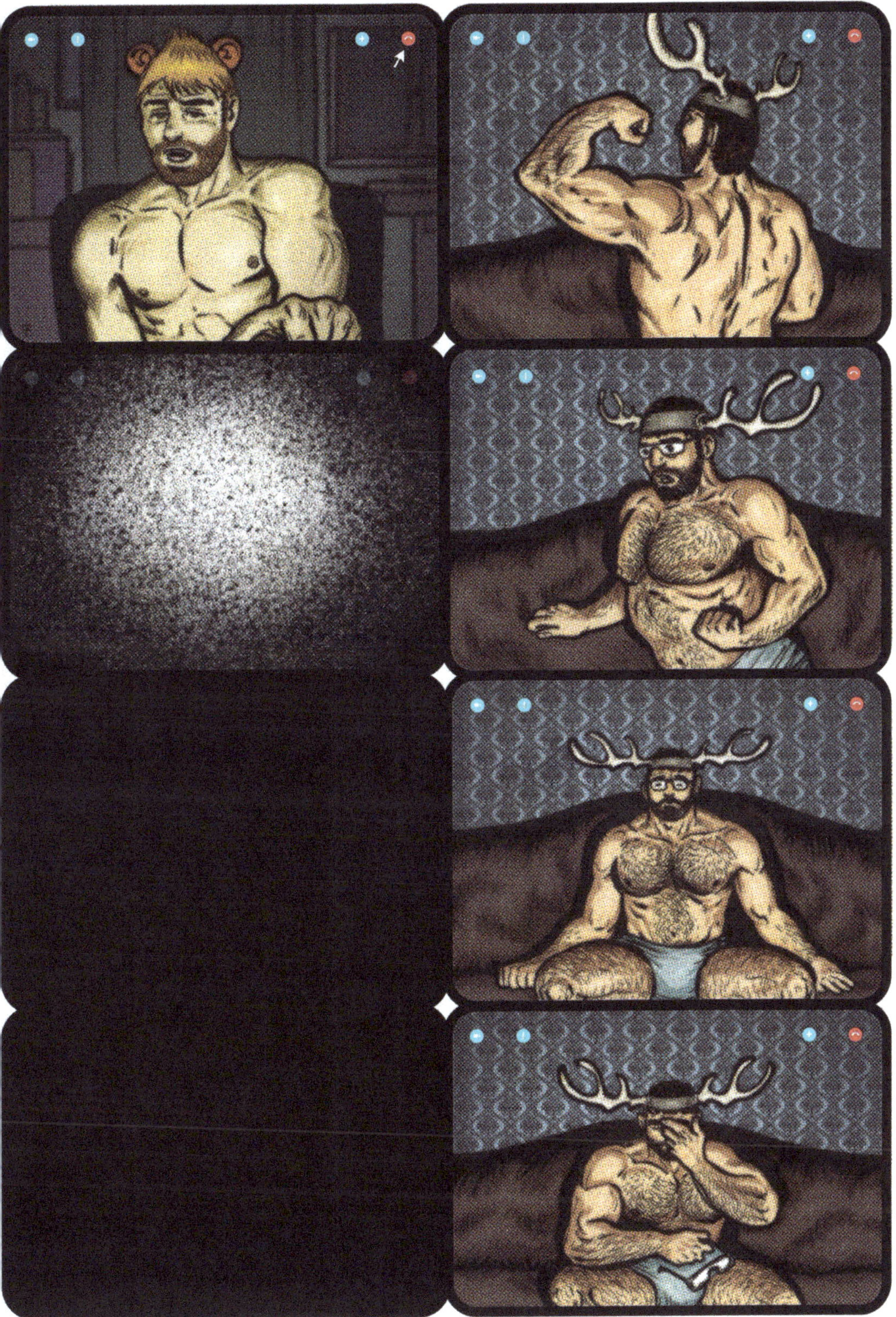

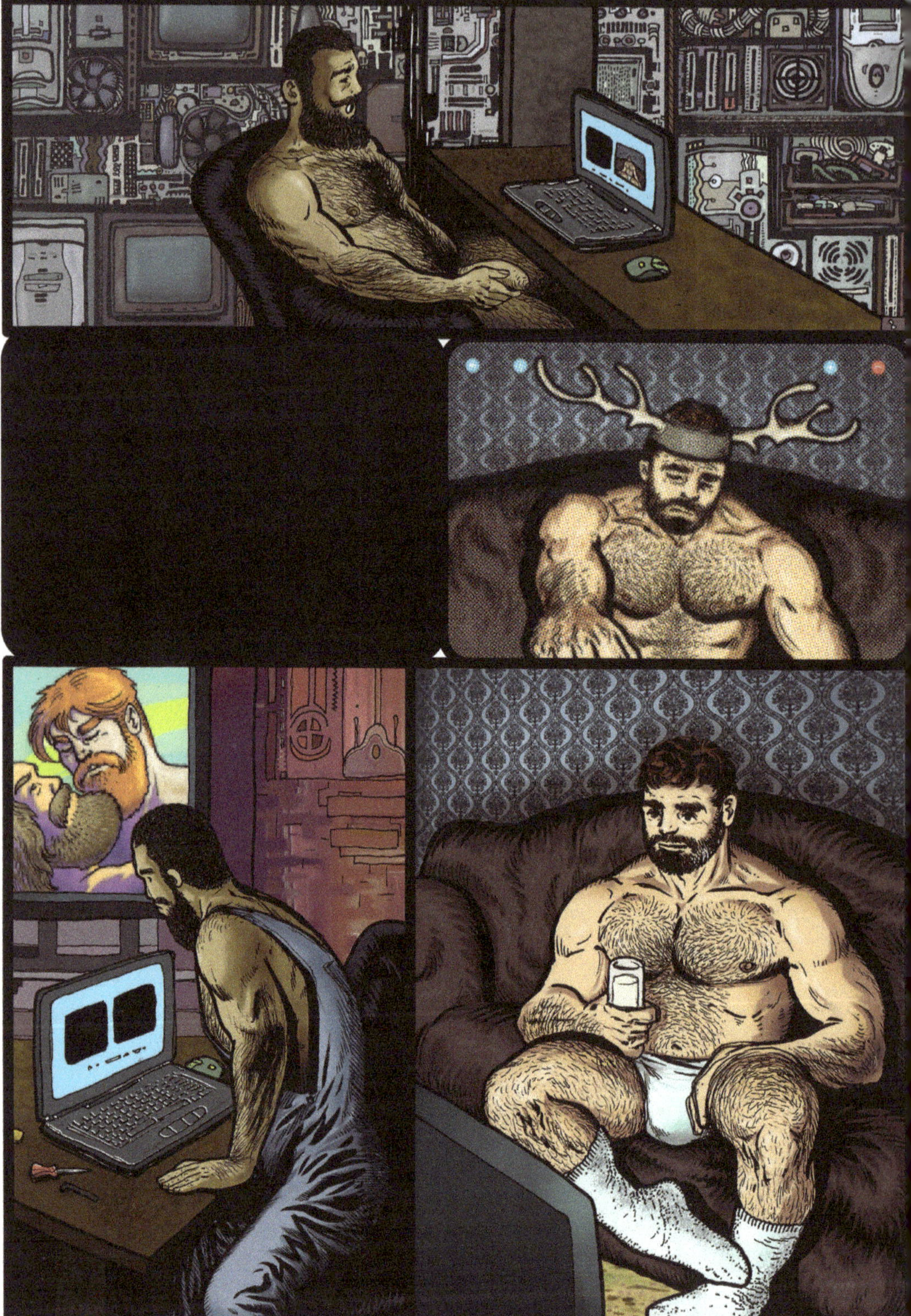

DALE
THE AMIR

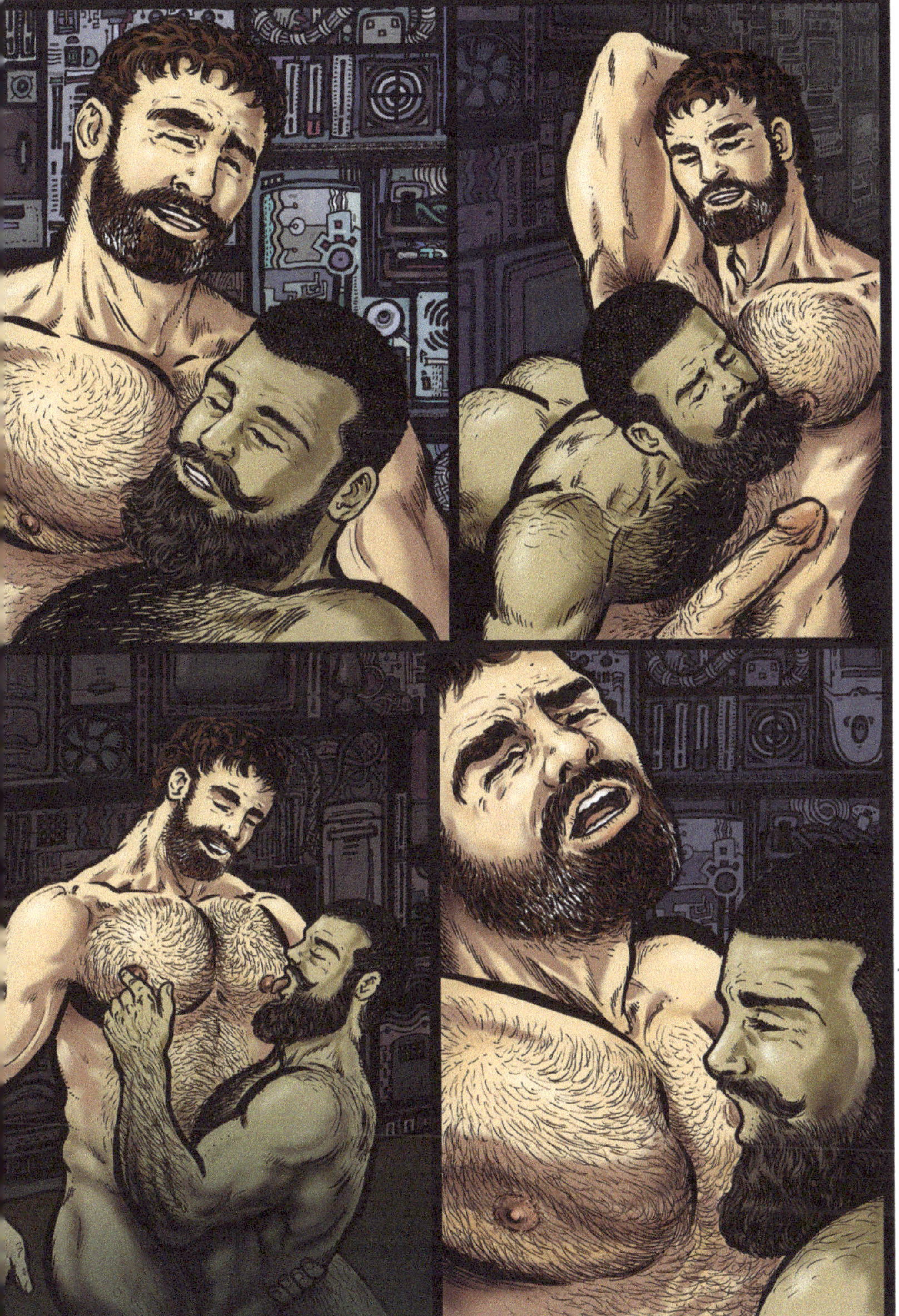

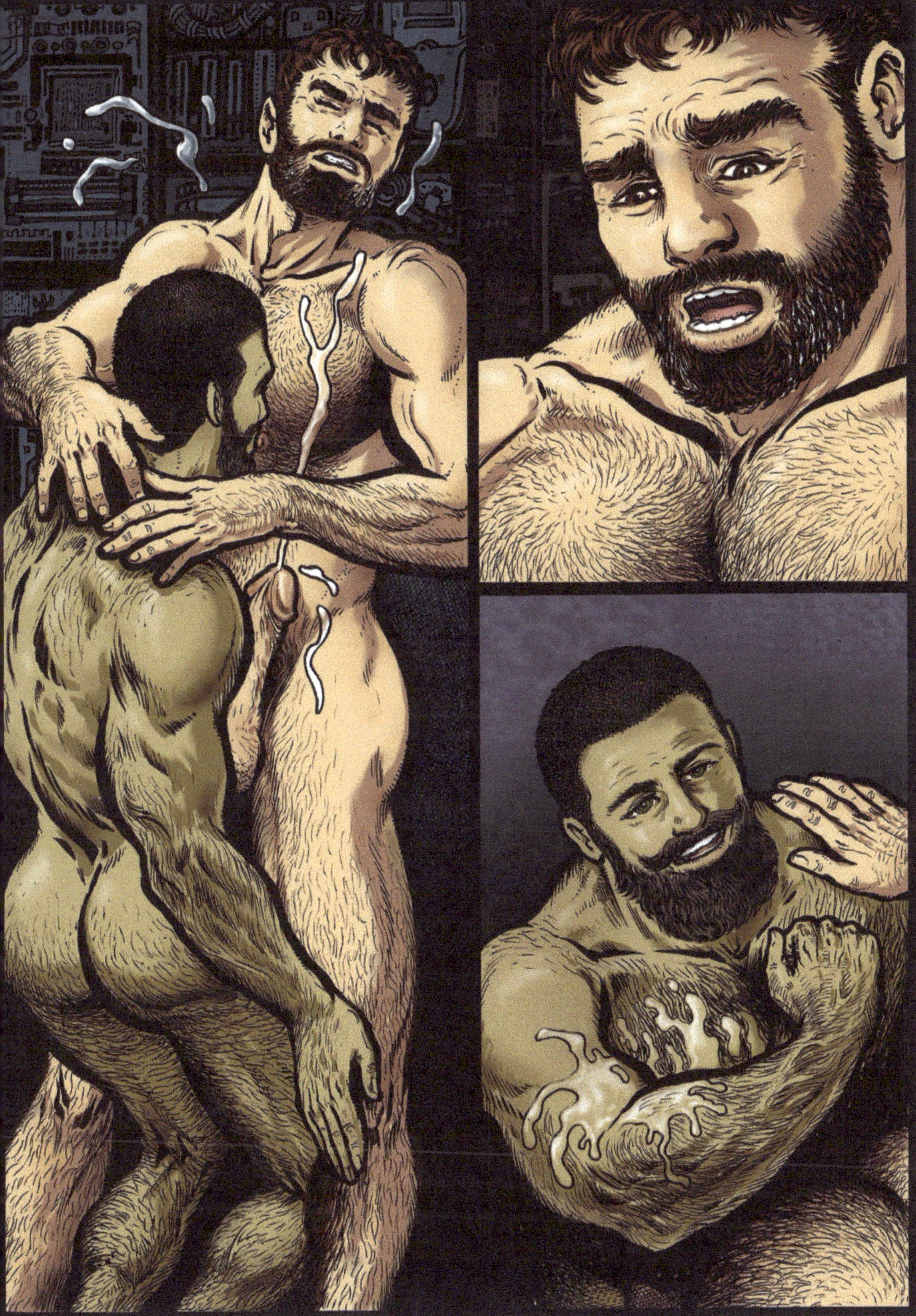

20

21

CONNECTING

CARNAL

script/art direction: Dale Lazarov
linework and colors: TheAmir

About The Authors:

Dale Lazarov is the writer/art director of TIMBER (drawn by Player), SLY (drawn by mpMann), BULLDOGS (drawn by Chas Hunter & Si Arden), PARDNERS (drawn by Bo Revel), PEACOCK PUNKS (drawn by Mauro Mariotti), FAST FRIENDS (drawn by Michael Broderick), GREEK LOVE (drawn by Adam Graphite), GOOD SPORTS (drawn by Alessio Slonimsky), NIGHTLIFE (drawn by Bastian Jonsson), MANLY (drawn by Amy Colburn), and STICKY (drawn by Steve MacIsaac) – wordless, gay character-based, sex-positive graphic novels published in hardcover by Comicmix and in digital format through Class Comics. He lives in Chicago.

TheAmir's early career as an erotic illustrator focused on BDSM and fetish painting. Currently, he explores the world of gay men from social, playful, psychological, spiritual, narrative and artistic points of view. He combines expressive traditional and digital strategies and techniques in his composition and illustration. He considers sexuality (and particularly homosexuality and "kinky sex") a rich universe to discover and to draw out of the social and cultural invisibility where it's still held as a prisoner. He currently pursues painting, illustration, comics art, calligraphy and manuscript illumination, writing, songwriting and singing. He feels old but, as a child, he was older, so he hopes to be born sooner or later.

StickyGraphicNovels.com

www.ingramcontent.com/pod-product-compliance
Lightning Source LLC
LaVergne TN
LVHW070146120826
845154LV00018B/17
* 9 7 8 1 9 3 9 8 8 8 5 3 2 *